Usborne Farmyard Tales

Poppy and Sam's
Favourite
Fairy Tales

This is a book of fairy tales that Poppy and Sam love. You might know them too, but they're going to be a little different this time. Watch out for the big bad wolf!

Usborne Farmyard Tales

Poppy and Sam's Favourite Fairy Tales

Retold by Laura Cowan

Illustrated by Stephen Cartwright

Additional illustrations by Simon Taylor-Kielty

Designed by Carly Davies, Reuben Barrance
and Sam Whibley

 Look out for a little yellow duck on every page.

Contents

Cinderella

Once there was a young woman named Cinderella. But her sisters, Dolores and Ava, called her Cinders. They thought it was funny.

"You're always covered in dirty cinders!" they sneered. That was because Cinderella was always working. Scrubbing, washing, dusting – her mother and sisters had many jobs for her to do.

It was very tiring indeed. But being a kind and hardworking person, she was happy to help. Her family was very busy and important after all. Or so they kept saying.

By bedtime, Cinderella just wanted to sleep. It was a good thing really. She'd have been quite lonely otherwise. Her family didn't seem to like her very much and they never wanted to talk – except about themselves.

One morning Dolores and Ava received a terribly exciting invitation.

"We've been invited to a ball tonight!" squealed Dolores. "By the Prince himself! We're going to the palace, Ava!"

Well actually Cinderella was invited too. But as her sisters pointed out, she had far too much work to do.

A ball sounds like fun...

"You need to style my wig!" said Ava. "And help me into my dress. And I can't tie my own ribbons, my fingers are too delicate."

It was a lot of work getting Dolores and Ava ready. There were so many ribbons and bows to tie. And their wigs were so tall they nearly touched the ceiling. But in the end they were ready to go.

"If you want, you can clean my room while I'm out,"
Ava told Cinderella as she left. Cinderella kept smiling.
She felt very small and sad inside though. When she had
finally finished all her work, she sat down to rest by the
fire. The house was silent... until **POOF!** ...a purple-
haired lady stood before her.

"I'm your fairy godmother, Cinderella! And you
SHALL go to the ball!"

Cinderella was so exhausted she barely looked up.

"Really? But I don't have anything to wear and it will take me too long to walk there now!"

"Leave that to me. I am a fairy after all." Her godmother twinkled, "All I need is a pumpkin from the vegetable garden, those mice in the trap and... are there any lizards out there? Maybe a rat? I think I could do a little something with a rat..."

Are you sure you want these?

Just you wait...

And she did! With a **WHOOSH** of her wand, the pumpkin grew and grew until it was a sparkling carriage. **SWOOSH!** The rat became the carriage driver.

PING-PING-PING-PING-PING-PING!

The six mice from the trap turned into six shining white horses. And as for the lizards, they sprouted into six tall footmen.

"Oh my gosh," said Cinderella, "you really are a fairy! All this could belong to a princess or even a queen."

"Well of course," her godmother replied, "I am pretty magical."

"If only I had something clean to wear,"
Cinderella sighed.

"Something clean? We can do better than that..."

SWISH! Cinderella's plain old work clothes became a
beautiful silk ballgown. She even had pink silk gloves and
ribbons to match. And some incredible glass slippers.

What about...

Wow!

"Oh! And do remember my magic only lasts till midnight,"
said the fairy, "so make sure you're home in plenty of time!"

Meanwhile the Prince was a bit bored. And at his own ball! It was full of silly people with some very silly things to say. But then... a mysterious woman in white arrived. Even her own sisters didn't recognize her. (It was Cinderella of course.) The Prince asked her to dance at once. She didn't dance that well, but she and the Prince spoke for hours. Until...

DONG, DONG, DONG...

... the clock was striking midnight. Cinderella didn't have a moment to lose! She shot out of the ballroom and flew downstairs as fast as she could – so fast that she lost one glass slipper on the stairs. (Glass is very hard to run in.)

Wait!

The Prince tried to follow, but Cinderella had already disappeared into the night.

Cinderella had to run all the way home – the magic had stopped working, just as her godmother had warned. And she couldn't ride a pumpkin!

She got back just in time for her sisters to walk through the door...

"Have you made our beds? We're absolutely exhausted."

Who WAS
that woman?

The next day, the Prince was staring at Cinderella's glass
slipper. He had never met anyone he could talk to so easily.
But no one knew who she was and she had completely
disappeared.

"I'll go to every single house in the kingdom," he said, "and
ask every single woman to try the slipper on."

When the Prince walked into Cinderella's house
with the slipper, her sisters were delighted.

"It looks like mine, doesn't it Dolores?"

"I think you'll find it's mine," said Dolores jamming
her toes in.

"I'm not sure it quite fits," the Prince frowned.
"What about your sister?"

"She's really more of a servant..." Dolores started, but
Cinderella was already slipping her foot in.

"It fits perfectly!" the Prince declared. His face was
beaming.

"But that's impossible!" cried Dolores and Ava.

WHOOSH! The fairy godmother appeared.

"Not quite," she chuckled. "Watch this..." **POOF!**

With a flourish of the fairy's wand, Cinderella was in
her beautiful ballgown again. Her sisters' mouths
fell open.

"It IS you!" cried the Prince. "I don't understand..."

"It's quite hard to explain..." Cinderella began.

"Well, if you don't mind, I'd love to get to know you
better," the Prince replied. "Would you like to join me for
some lunch at the palace?"

"Thank you, I really would," smiled Cinderella.
"We have so much to talk about!"
And off they went.

Little Red Riding Hood

Once upon a time there was a little girl named Ivy, who lived with her mother in a cottage by the woods. Ivy's granny had made her a red cape for her birthday, and Ivy loved it. "From now on," she declared, "I want to be called by my superhero name – Red Riding Hood, or Red for short."

One afternoon, Red was in the kitchen, watching her mother pack up a picnic basket full of delicious food.

"Ivy, I mean, Red, will you take this to your grandmother's? She's been unwell and I think a good meal would help."
"Red Riding Hood to the rescue!" shouted Red.

Before her mother even had time to say STAY ON THE PATH, Red had put on her cape and set off with the basket. Her grandmother lived right in the middle of the woods and it was a long, dark path to her home. Luckily Red's mother had sent the dog after her. Not that Red needed any help – she was Red Riding Hood after all!

Red was enjoying her walk, when she came across a great slobbering wolf sitting on the path. The dog took one look and shot off in the opposite direction.

"Oh hello little girl," said the wolf. Red frowned.

"I'm not a little girl," she said, "I'm Red Riding Hood."

"LITTLE Red Riding Hood more like," scoffed the wolf. "You're the size of a PEBBLE to me."

"Well actually I'm a superhero. Can't you see my cape?" Red replied. The wolf ignored her.

"Where are you going, little girl?" he asked. "What are you carrying in that nice basket? It smells yummy." And so do you, he thought.

"I'm on an important mission," said Red. "I'm taking my granny this food. She's not very well and she lives right in the middle of these woods you see."

Without even bothering to reply, the wolf bounded off
along the path.

"Hmph! What a rude wolf," Red said to herself, "and
where's that cowardly dog? Well, never mind, I think
I'll pick Granny some of these flowers. That'll cheer
her up."

Meanwhile the wolf had run so fast that he was already outside Granny's house. He peered in the window and saw the little old lady reading in bed.

Ever so softly he nudged the front door open with his nose and padded over to the bed. Then with one enormous LEAP, he snatched up Red's granny and shut her in the cellar!

"I'm getting hungry," the wolf said to no one in particular, "but that little girl will be here soon. I think I'll eat her and Granny together. Ah, I know what to do..."

The wolf put on Granny's glasses, cap and nightdress and climbed into her bed. He pulled her quilt up to his snout and settled in to wait.

Soon enough Red knocked on the door. But there was no answer. She knocked again. This time a tiny little voice called out...

"Oh hello dear, is that you, my sweet little granddaughter? I'm in bed, but the door's open!"

Red frowned. Granny knew she wasn't a sweet little girl.

She was Red Riding Hood, a brave, strong superhero. But Granny wasn't feeling well, so maybe she'd forgotten. Red pushed the door open.

"STOP!" growled a deep voice, then the little voice started again. "I mean wait! I need to explain something. I'm very ill indeed. So I might look a little strange."

Red squinted. Maybe it was just a different nightie, but Red could have sworn Granny was furry. She took a step closer.

"But Granny, what big ears you have!"

Red dropped her flowers in surprise.

"All the better to hear you with," squeaked the wolf.

"And Granny, what big eyes you have!"

"All the better to see you with..."

"But Granny, what big TEETH you have..."

"All the better to EAT you with!" growled the wolf and leaped out of the bed, shutting Red in the cellar too! **SLAM!** The wolf was so pleased with himself, he decided he needed a little rest before dinner and soon fell fast asleep.

But little did he know that Red's dog was coming to the rescue. He had found a woodcutter and didn't stop barking until the poor man followed him – all the way to Granny's house. No one answered the woodcutter's knock.

So he pushed open the door to find a gigantic snoring wolf on the bed. The dog scampered past him and began to howl at the cellar door. "HELP!" Red called.

The woodcutter smashed open the cellar door to see
Granny and Red huddled together. The dog sprang into
Red's arms. Meanwhile the woodcutter gave the wolf a good
knock on the head so he wouldn't wake up for a while. Red
helped Granny back to bed.

"I really don't understand what happened!" Granny said.
"Where are my glasses?"

Red picked them carefully off the stunned wolf's snout
and passed them to her confused granny.

"Well, Granny, this man is a superhero too and he's saved us both from a HORRIBLE wolf."

"Woof, woof!" said the dog.

"Yes, you helped too," laughed Red.

"Well, I can't think of a better way to thank you BOTH than sharing this basket of delicious food," Red's granny said. So they did.

Sleeping Beauty

Once upon a time, a king and queen had a baby daughter. When Princess Zara was born, they were the happiest they'd ever been.

"Let's throw a party," said the Queen, "I want everyone to be as happy as we are." So they invited all the people from miles around, and the six fairies in their kingdom too.

We need to celebrate!

There were actually SEVEN fairies in the kingdom, but no one had seen the seventh one for many years. In fact the Queen thought she'd probably gone away, so she didn't even try to invite her.

"We'd be so happy if you'd be godmothers to our Princess Zara," the King said to the six fairies at the party. The fairies flittered and fluttered their wings in delight.

"Oh how lovely," they said. "And we will each give her a present." You might think presents means toys, but these were fairies, so their presents were magical.

"I give her courage!" said one. **WHOOSH!**

"I give her kindness!" said another. **WHOOSH!** Five fairies gave magical gifts like this, but then there was a **CRACK** of thunder and the seventh fairy appeared. The one everyone had forgotten about. Drusilla. She hadn't left the kingdom after all.

"Oh, you're all here, are you?" said Drusilla. "Everyone was invited, EXCEPT ME. Just because I'm not cute and tiny. Well, I have a gift, too.

It's actually more of a curse. When the princess is sixteen, she will prick her finger on a spinning wheel and fall asleep FOREVER." **CRACK!** The spell was cast.

The fairies started screaming and wailing. But the sixth fairy Aziza stepped forward.

"Wait!" said Aziza, "I haven't given my gift yet. I can't break Drusilla's curse, but I can soften it. She won't fall asleep forever – one day she'll wake up again." **WHOOSH!**

The other fairies told the King and Queen what had happened.

"What are we going to do?" the Queen cried.

"Well, that's easy," said the King. "She can't prick her finger if there are no spinning wheels in the kingdom! I command they all be burned."

And so they were. It was quite annoying for everyone who lived there as they had to buy all their spun wool from the kingdom next door.

Nearly sixteen years went by and Princess Zara grew up with all the fairies' gifts and more. No one ever spoke about Drusilla's curse. They thought it was best to pretend it hadn't happened. It wasn't going to come true. Or so they thought. But of course that's not how magic works...

On the morning of her sixteenth birthday, Zara woke up early and went for a walk around the palace. She found a staircase she was sure she'd never seen before.

"How strange," said Zara, "I wonder where this goes."

Where am I?

She went up and up until she reached a door at the top and pushed it open. There she found an old woman spinning.

46

"Hello? What are you doing?" asked Zara. She'd never seen a spinning wheel before.

"It's called spinning," said Drusilla (because of course that's who it really was). "Would you like to try it?"

"I'd love to," Zara said. "What do I do?"

"First you need to touch this needle," said the fairy with a sickly sweet smile. Zara reached out with her finger.

"Ouch!" She dropped to the floor – fast asleep.

Just press there.

And it wasn't just Zara. The whole palace fell into a deep, deep sleep. Except for the fairies.

"We should have known," said Aziza sadly. "Magic always finds a way. Or at least Drusilla does." The fairies carried Zara back to her bedroom and placed her gently on the bed.

"But how long will they sleep?" asked one.

"It's hard to say," Aziza shrugged, "Drusilla's magic is strong. We'll just have to keep the palace safe until they all wake up again."

So the fairies cast spells to protect the sleeping palace. They made the forest grow thick around it so no one would even know it was there. They grew great big thorny thickets to put off any passersby from exploring. Soon the palace and everyone inside was hidden from the rest of the world. And that's how it stayed for a long, long time.

One afternoon, many years later, a prince named Riz was walking his dog in that very same forest. He'd heard that there was once a palace there, at the heart of a great kingdom, but no one had been inside it for a hundred years. As he strolled among the trees, he met an old man.

You'll never get in.

"The palace?" the old man said when Riz asked. "My grandfather told me the forest grew suddenly and after that no one heard from that palace ever again. But that sounds like a fairy tale to me."

Fairy tale or no fairy tale, Riz could see the palace over the tops of the trees. He pushed his way through the thicket, until he found a gatehouse. The door was unlocked.

"This must be it," Riz said to his dog.

He walked through into a courtyard and saw the palace surrounded by sleeping guards.

"So, it is real," gasped Riz and ran up the steps.

He passed many more people, fast asleep – some quiet, some snoring – and followed a staircase up to a huge room. Inside, a girl of his own age was fast asleep.

"This is so strange," said Riz. "Hello?" He gently shook her shoulders. The girl stirred. Then she yawned and sat up.

"Hello?" she said. "Who are you?"

"I'm Prince Riz, who are you?"

"I'm Princess Zara. I've never heard of you before," she said.

"And I've never heard of you!" said Riz. "I think you've been asleep for a long time."

Meanwhile the rest of the palace was waking up.

Aziza and the other fairies flew from room to room, explaining what had happened. Then they all went outside to look at the overgrown forest.

"We should throw a party to thank Prince Riz for waking me up!" said Princess Zara.

"Good idea!" Aziza replied. "But let's invite Drusilla this time? If you don't want to sleep for another hundred years!"

Three Little Pigs

O nce upon a time there were three little pigs. They lived with their mother in a tiny little cottage. It was so little that they all kept bumping into each other. So one day Mother Pig said...

"My dear little pigs, unfortunately you're not piglets anymore. You're great big piggies and it's time for you to go out into the world and find your own homes."

The three little pigs knew their mother was right. It was time. So they packed up their belongings and set off down the garden path.

"Good luck, my dears," their mother called. "Come back soon. And watch out for the big bad wolf!"

The first little piggy set off on his own and soon bumped into a farmer with a MASSIVE bale of straw.

"Straw is light and easy to carry," the piggy said to himself.

"OINK! May I buy your straw?" he asked the farmer. "May I buy enough to build a house?"

The farmer wasn't sure that straw was good for building houses, but he sold the little piggy as much as he wanted.

He even told him where there was an empty field. So the piggy wove himself a beautiful little home from all the straw and was very pleased with himself indeed. So pleased that he never noticed the big bad wolf lurking behind his hedge...

The second little pig had taken another road. After a
while, he came across a woodcutter with a huge bundle
of sticks on his back. This little piggy thought himself
very clever.

"With that many sticks I could build myself my own
cottage!" said the piggy to himself. "OINK!"

"I'll take the lot!" he said.

BASH! BASH! BANG! BANG! SAW!

It took him a little longer than his brother, but in the end he'd built himself a lovely little cottage made of sticks. He put some cheerful curtains over the window and he was quite happy with his new home. The big bad wolf looking over his hedge thought it was very nice too.

Now you're probably wondering what had happened to the third little pig? Well on the road she'd chosen, she came across a bricklayer with a great big barrow of bricks.

"Oh!" said the little piggy. "Bricks! Now I've read about these and they make absolutely the strongest and safest houses you can build. I'll take them all!"

So she did. The bricklayer even sold her some tiles for her roof and glass for her windows. Then the little piggy went straight to the library to take out some books on building houses. It took her a long time to finish her cottage. But at last it was done.

"It's PERFECT," she oinked to herself.

That's what YOU think...

Not one of the little piggies had remembered to watch out for the big bad wolf. So the first little pig was quite surprised when he looked through his window and saw the wolf at his door.

"I'll HUFF and I'll PUFF and I'll BLOW your house down," shouted the wolf.

"But why!?" squealed the scared little pig.

"Just because it's FUN," the wolf snarled.

And so he HUFFED and he PUFFED and he blew the straw house clean away. **SWISH!**

The first little piggy rushed to his brother's house and told him what had happened.

"Well, of course you can stay here," the second piggy said. But it wasn't long before they heard a huff and a puff, and when they looked out between the curtains, who do you think was there? The big bad wolf of course.

"I'll HUFF and I'll PUFF, and I'll BLOW your house DOWN," said the wolf.

And so he HUFFED and he PUFFED and he DID
blow the house down. **WHOOSH!** It was harder than
blowing a straw house down, but not by much.

"But why!?" cried the piggies.

"Because I felt like it," said the wolf. The scared piggies
ran to their sister's house as fast as they could.

"Quick, come inside and I'll lock the door," said the third piggy. They rushed inside and sat in silence for a moment, when... **KNOCK, KNOCK**.

"I'll HUFF and I'll PUFF and I'll BLOW your house down too," crowed the wolf. So he huffed. Nothing happened. And he puffed. STILL nothing happened.

He huffed and puffed again. The house didn't move a single inch.

"Hmmm," said the wolf. "Well, I'm going to come inside and smash up all your nice things instead." He bounded onto the roof and sniffed around the chimney. Maybe he could fit down it.

Good thing I'm so slim..!

"What are we going to do?" cried the first pig.

"I'm scared!" the second pig grunted. But the third pig put a big pan of soapy water on the stove. And SPLOSH! ...the wolf fell straight in.

"WAH! I hate being clean!" howled the wolf, leaping into the air and running straight out of the house.

"That'll teach you, you big bully!" said the third piggy.

"Thank you, sister," squealed the first two piggies. "You're so brave! Can we stay with you?"

"Well you have to stand up to bullies," she replied with an OINK. "And you can stay as long as you like. I'll help you build new homes - and this time we'll use bricks! But first I think we all deserve a nice cup of tea."

Oink!   Grunt!

Rumpelstiltskin

There once was a young woman named Helga. She lived with her father in a windmill miles from anywhere. It was a hard life and not very interesting. So when she heard the King himself would be passing their windmill, she knew she had to meet him. She made her father wait outside with her.

"Your highness, I'm very talented," said Helga, "I could work at the palace! I can do anything!"

"Hello, yes, very nice," the King said with a wave, not really listening.

"I can make a hundred beds in an hour! I can spin straw into gold!" yelled Helga. The King stopped. Being able to turn straw into gold sounded fantastic. This could make him even richer!

"Really? Come back to the palace and show me then."

Uh oh...

So Helga found herself locked in a room at the palace with nothing but a spinning wheel and an enormous pile of straw she had to turn into gold by morning.

"Oops," said Helga. "How am I going to get out of this?"

"Hello there!" said a strange little man as he danced into the room. "I think I can help you."

"Can you spin straw into gold?" Helga asked.

"I can," said the man, "if you give me that lovely necklace you're wearing..."

"Well, I don't have much choice, do I?" said Helga, "It's a deal." The little man sat down at the wheel and began to spin. Helga tried to watch but after all the excitement of the day she quickly fell asleep. When she woke the next morning, both the straw and the man were gone and a pile of gold sat next to the wheel.

"Wow," said the King when he saw it, "can you do this pile too?"

"Of course I can!" lied Helga. "Easy peasy!"

"I don't know if this is better or worse," she said to herself. "Now the King really believes I'm magic!"

But no sooner was Helga alone, than the little man appeared again.

"I'm happy to help," he said. "The deal is you give me that nice ring on your finger."

Now this ring had belonged to Helga's mother, so she didn't want to give it away. But she didn't have a choice.

The next morning, the man was gone and so was the straw. In its place was a huge pile of gold.

"This really is fantastic," said the King. "I don't know if I've ever seen such a big pile of gold – and I'm a king! Are you a fairy? You look too big!"

"I'm just really talented," said Helga.

The King led her to another room. Here the pile of straw was so enormous, it almost brushed the ceiling.

"If you can turn this into gold, I'm going to be richer than any other king I know."

Helga thought about it.

"I can do that, your highness. But I want something in return. I want..." Helga said slowly, "I want to be queen and rule the kingdom with you."

So this one's quite big...

The King was surprised, but he thought about it for a moment.

"Well, do you know, it's actually very hard being king all on my own. It's a deal!"

That night Helga waited for the man to come back. When he popped up again, she was ready.

"I can't pay you now," said Helga, "but if you turn this pile of straw into gold, I'll become queen and then I'll be rich."

This is one LARGE pile of straw...

Yes, but can you do it?

"Well," said the little man slowly, "I'm lonely. So, when you have a baby, I would like it to come and live with me."

"Is that all?" thought Helga. "I might never have a baby, so it doesn't matter."

"It's a deal," she said.

The next morning, the man was gone, and the biggest pile of gold ANYONE had ever seen was there. "This is amazing!" said the King. "You're so talented, Helga, you're going to be great at running the kingdom!"

So Helga became a queen. And many years later when she and the King knew each other a lot better, they fell in love, got married, and even had a little baby. Helga never thought much about how she became queen.

But one night, when she was rocking her baby to sleep, who should appear in the nursery, but the strange little man. "I've come to collect my baby," he said.

"Don't be silly!" cried Helga, "I can pay you properly now. I told you – I'm a queen!"

"But I want my own baby," the little man said. "You promised." Helga started to cry. She couldn't just give him her child.

"Alright, alright," the man frowned. "Here's a new deal. If you can guess my name, the baby stays with you. I'll give you three nights." How hard could it be? thought Helga.

"Craig, Sayeed, Keegan, Norris...." she began.

"No, no, no, no," said the little man, very pleased with himself indeed. By morning Helga couldn't think of any more names and none of her guesses had been right.

So she sent out messengers all over the kingdom to try and find out about the little man. Someone somewhere must know him! But by the afternoon of the third day, not one had found a trace of him. Until one messenger came back.

"Your highness! I was riding through the mountains when I passed a strange little man singing in his garden about how the queen would never guess his name. But I saw it on his letter box – it said RUMPELSTILTSKIN!"

When the little man returned that evening, quite a few people had gathered to watch.

"Is your name Leonard? Ian? Or is it Kwame?" asked Helga.

"Wrong, wrong, wrong," said Rumpelstiltskin.

"What about... RUMPELSTILTSKIN?" Helga smiled.

"HOW COULD YOU POSSIBLY KNOW?" Rumpelstiltskin shrieked, stamping his foot. He stamped so hard, his foot went through the stone floor and got stuck.

"Oh dear," said the King, trying not to laugh, "it's a good thing you spun us enough gold to buy a new floor!"

Goldilocks
and the Three Bears

BEAR
COTTAGE

Once there were three bears who lived in a little cottage in the forest – Father Bear, Mother Bear and their little Baby Bear. They had spent a lot of time making their home as lovely as they could.

"It's the neatest, tidiest house in the whole forest," beamed Mother Bear.

One morning, Father Bear had made everyone porridge (as he always did) and Mother Bear spooned it into their bowls (as she always did). She added a little salt to Father's and a little honey to Baby Bear's. Just the way they liked it.

"It's nine o'clock!" announced Father Bear. "Time for our morning walk while the porridge cools down."

And so they set off. But little did they know that someone else was on a morning walk too – a small girl named Goldilocks. She definitely wasn't allowed to go for walks alone, but Goldilocks didn't care about what she was ALLOWED to do. So when she came across the bears' home in the forest, she couldn't resist looking through the windows. "I wonder who lives here," said Goldilocks, trying the door, which Father Bear had left unlocked (as he always did).

The smell of delicious porridge wafted out.

"Mmmm, maybe I'll have a little taste..." she said, sneaking in and helping herself to a spoonful from Daddy Bear's bowl.

"Ugh, who puts SALT in their porridge?" said Goldilocks, throwing the spoon down in disgust.

Mother Bear's porridge didn't taste of anything, but Baby Bear's was just right and Goldilocks slurped it all up.

"BURP! Now for a little sit down," said Goldilocks, plopping herself into Father Bear's chair. "OW, this is far too hard."

She got up straight away and spied Mother Bear's comfy armchair. But she didn't like that either.

"OOF! It feels like I'm sinking!" Goldilocks complained.

But there was still Baby Bear's little green seat to try.

Now Goldilocks was a bit bigger than Baby Bear and quite a lot heavier. She sat down on his small seat and...

CRASH! The chair's legs shuddered and gave way. Goldilocks was on the floor!

"OOPS!" she said.

Stupid chair!

"Well, that was VERY scary," said Goldilocks. "I could have HURT myself. I deserve a rest after that."

She scampered upstairs to the bedroom to find Father
Bear's big blue bed. She lay down without even taking her
shoes off. "OUCH!" she bellowed. "This isn't comfy at all!"
Mother Bear's pink bed looked inviting, but...

"UGH! It's sucking me in!"
So Goldilocks clambered out and looked around.

"One more to try," she said, pulling the covers back on Baby Bear's bed. She climbed in with her dirty shoes and lay her head on Baby Bear's soft pillow.

"Oo, I love this bed," she said. "It's so comfy. I'll just shut my eyes for a second..."

And very soon, Goldilocks was fast asleep and snoring like a train.

Downstairs, the bear family had returned and they were not happy at all.

"I think someone's been eating my porridge," said Father Bear in a puzzled voice.

"Someone's left a spoon in mine," said Mother Bear, equally puzzled.

Baby Bear looked at his bowl and started to cry.
"Someone's been eating my porridge too," he sobbed,
"and they've eaten it all up."

"How awful!" said Father Bear.

"But who could it be?" asked Mother.

Then Father Bear noticed something else.

"Someone's been sitting in my chair," he said. "My cushion has someone else's bottom print in it!"

Father Bear didn't like this one little bit. (As you know, the bear family liked their home to be just right.)

Mother Bear looked across the room and gasped.

"Someone's been sitting in MY chair!" she said. "There's a big dent in the middle."

Tearful Baby Bear found the remains of his little green chair and cried even harder.

"Sss-ss-someone's been sitting in my chair," he howled, "an-an-and they've BROKEN it!"

"Our beautiful little home!" Father Bear cried. "It's RUINED!"

"But who would do such a thing?" Mother Bear wondered.

Suddenly the sound of loud snoring drifted down from the bedroom. The bears rushed up the stairs.

"Somebody's been sleeping in my bed!" said Father Bear. "The covers are all crumpled!"

"How peculiar," said Mother Bear. "Somebody's been sleeping in MY bed."

She shook out her blankets.

Baby Bear was still sniffling. He shuffled over to his bed and shrieked!

"Somebody's been sleeping in my bed," cried Baby Bear, "AND SHE'S STILL THERE!"

Goldilocks sat up with a jolt. When she opened her eyes, three huge bears were staring at her angrily. Well, one was smaller but it was still... A BEAR.

"DON'T EAT ME!" she screamed. Springing out of the bed, she ran down the stairs as fast as she could.

She ran straight through the kitchen, out of the front door, through the forest and all the way home. And she never ever came back.

The bears spent the rest of the day making their home beautiful again. And Father Bear never ever left the door unlocked, just in case.

Cover illustration by Simon Taylor-Kielty
Edited by Sam Taplin
Additional designs by Kate Rimmer
Digital manipulation: Keith Furnival

This edition first published in 2021 by Usborne Publishing Ltd,
Usborne House, 83-85 Saffron Hill, London EC1N 8RT, England.
usborne.com Copyright © 2021, 2006, 2004, 1989-1996 Usborne Publishing Ltd.